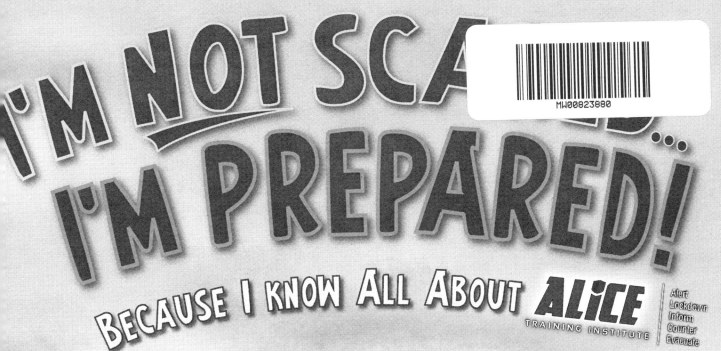

I'M NOT SCARED... I'M PREPARED!

BECAUSE I KNOW ALL ABOUT ALICE
TRAINING INSTITUTE

Alert
Lockdown
Inform
Counter
Evacuate

Activity & Idea Book

published by

National Center for Youth Issues
Youth Issues
ncyi.org
Practical Guidance Resources
Educators Can Trust

Introduction

ALICE (Alert, Lockdown, Inform, Counter, Evacuate) is a comprehensive program which addresses communication technology, building infrastructure, and citizen training to build survival strategies for a violent intruder event.

The purpose of this book is to enhance the concepts taught in the **ALICE Training** and make them applicable to children of all ages in a non-fearful way. By using this book along with Julia Cook's *I'm Not Scared...Cause I'm Prepared!* story book, children can develop a better understanding of what needs to be done if they ever encounter a "dangerous someone." Unfortunately in the world we now live in, we all must ask ourselves the essential question: **What options do I have for survival, if I ever find myself in a violent intruder event?**

TOOL BOX and Activity Book Objectives:

- Define "The Wolf" or a "dangerous someone" as a person that isn't supposed to be in the school building.
- Listen to directions and follow the teacher's safety signal without question.
- Evacuate to a "Special Meeting Place" or "Rally Point."
- Understand that evacuation or getting out of harm's way, if it is safe to do so, is the desired response.
- Demonstrate LOCKDOWN skills including being quiet, staying out of plain sight (without hiding where movement may be restricted), spreading out around the room, having something in hand to throw, and seeing windows as a possible point of escape.
- Demonstrate or model the skills of barricading a door.
- Demonstrate the use of movement, noise, distance and distractions, which are critical when coming into contact with an intruder or "The Wolf."
- Demonstrate the ability to move safely, quickly, and in a zig-zag pattern without running into one another using body and spatial awareness.
- Demonstrate the use of critical thinking skills to practice responding to a stimulus.
- Demonstrate the differences between an "inside" and "outside" voice and describe when it would be appropriate to use an "outside" voice while inside the building.
- Participate in drills and practices of ALICE for the purposes of skill development and mental preparation.

ADDITIONAL RESOURCES

U.S. Department of Education, et al. 2013. *Guide for Developing High-quality School Emergency Operations Plans.* http://rems.ed.gov

International Association of Chiefs of Police, 2009. *Guide for Preventing & Responding to School Violence.* http://www.theiacp.org/Prevention-And-Response-To-School-Violence

Federal Emergency Management Agency (FEMA) Training. IS-100. SCA: *Introduction to the Incident Command Systems for Schools.* http://www.fema.gov/national-incident-management-system

Duplication and Copyright

National Center for Youth Issues
Practical Guidance Resources
Educators Can Trust
ncyi.org

P.O. Box 22185 • Chattanooga, TN 37422-2185
423.899.5714 • 866.318.6294 • fax: 423.899.4547
www.ncyi.org

ISBN: 978-1-937870-31-7
© 2014 National Center for Youth Issues, Chattanooga, TN
All rights reserved.

Summary: A supplementary teacher's guide for *I'm Not Scared...I'm Prepared.* Full of discussion questions and exercises to share with students.

Written by: Julia Cook
Contributing Editor: Lisa J. Crane M.Ed.
Illustrations by: Michelle Hazelwood Hyde
Published by National Center for Youth Issues

Printed at Starkey Printing • Chattanooga, TN, USA
August 2014

10 Concepts of ALICE for Elementary

ALICE Training for the elementary aged child is age and ability appropriate. **ALICE Training Institute always leaves the grade level of implementation up to the local school district.**

1. Children should be taught to follow directions the first time they are given in an emergency. We don't want teachers to give directions for evacuate or lockdown and have students standing around asking, "But why?"

2. Students should be trained to **STOP, LOOK and LISTEN** to announcements at the time they are given. If the PA system serves as the main information source in a school, students must be trained to **STOP, LOOK and LISTEN** every time it comes on.

3. In a lockdown, be quiet, listen to directions, stay out of the line of sight from the door, but **DO NOT** hide in a closet. Be ready to move or evacuate if the intruder comes into the room.

4. In a counter situation when the secured location has been breached by an intruder, and evacuation is not possible, the best line of defense is to have kids up, moving, making noise, increasing distance and throwing items at the intruder.

5. Evacuation is the best defense, if the information indicates it is safe to do so. Parents, staff and students must know where the RALLY/REUNIFICATION point is located. This location is usually away and separate from the school. Students should know how to get to the RALLY/REUNIFICATION point from every part of the school, and how to move quickly **with OR without** the teacher. It should be emphasized to parents that the RALLY/REUNIFICATION point is the place to go in case of an emergency.

6. Upper elementary students have more developed critical thinking and problem solving skills and should take a much more active role in ALICE than children in the lower elementary grades.

7. Teach all aspects of ALICE **EXCEPT** the *"swarm technique"* (grabbing onto the appendages of an intruder and using your body weight to immobilize him) to elementary students.

8. Special needs students are planned for ahead of time, given their individualized situations. If a student cannot evacuate, plans must be made to fortify his/her location. When students with special needs are included in the general education class, teachers need to decide what is in the child's best interest and plans should be made ahead of time. There is not a *one-size-fits-all* answer to the situations involving a student with special needs. The school must consider each case individually.

9. Education and empowerment are the keys to preparation and relieving fear.

10. Kids are taught in realistic terms what to do in case of danger. ALICE is much like a fire drill or a tornado drill. Its purpose is to prepare students for life inside and out of the classroom. The ALICE concepts are the same at school, home, the mall, the afterschool program, restaurants, church or any other place the child goes. We are teaching a life-long safety skill.

HOW TO USE THIS BOOK

The activities in this book are divided into two sections. The first section (pages 6 through 18) are considered ESSENTIAL. They are important in solidifying the ALICE concepts. Please make sure that students complete these activities. The second section (pages 19 through 24) are "extracurricular" to support drills throughout the year.

"Go Bucket" Kit
Items to Keep in the Classroom

Items can be stored in a clean and preferably brightly-colored/well-marked five-gallon plastic bucket with handle and lid. The side and top should be stenciled or clearly labeled with classroom number/code for easy visual identification. An alternative would be a brightly colored backpack to allow a teacher to keep hands free during a crisis; it can also be hung on a hook just inside the classroom door. (One advantage of the bucket is that it can be emptied, lined with heavy-duty plastic bags such as are used for trash compactors, and used as an emergency toilet).

The "Go-Bucket" may go with the class during all emergency situations. Don't make it too heavy to carry; for grades K-4, think about splitting the items up by type among smaller containers, but ensure they are all kept in the same known location. Tape closed and "witness-mark" to reduce tampering or pilfering, and ward off "inquisitive little hands".

Examples shown. Please follow materials list.

"Go Buckets" can be augmented by every child also possessing a small "Go Pack", with items such as flashlight, disposable poncho, snack bar and personal medical information.

Please Note
1. Check and replenish the stock at the beginning of every semester or more often if possible.
2. Some items may have limited shelf life. Keep medicines and sharp objects secure in the container for safety.

Materials
- (5) Gallon Bucket
- Toilet Seat Cover (Bucket can double as a portable bathroom for emergency situations)
- Package of Toilet Bags
- Toilet paper
- Small first aid kit (bandages, tampons, gauze pads, iodine solution, sterile latex gloves, antiseptic cream, aspirin, Imodium, Benadryl, eye pads, burn dressings, antiseptic lotion)
- Feminine hygiene paper products that can double as gunshot wound/blood loss suppressors
- Emergency food (bars, pemmican/jerky)
- If the room has no water supply, then you should have bottled water stored in room.
- Hand-cleaning gel or wipes
- Small bottles of bleach and disinfectant
- A hat, vest, armband or other unique identifier for the teacher (and aide if applicable)
- A whistle
- Space blanket(s)
- Duct tape
- 2 or 3 large plastic trash bags
- Student class list; key medical information
- Age appropriate "Time Passers:" cards, games, etc.
- Flashlight with spare batteries
- Barricade aids (zip ties, rope, parachute cord, glass punch to break window)
- Current class lists with emergency contact information.

Laying Out Your Classroom

Teachers should be mindful about how they lay out their classrooms to maximize safety. Always keep in mind that an intruder will decide when and where he tries to start his mission.

Should your classroom become the first target, the way you have things arranged may assist you in the three-step threat process: Recognize, Assess, and Respond. You need time to do all three. Your classroom layout can provide you some time.

As the leader in the classroom, the teacher is usually the first target of the attacker. It is important to configure your classroom so you are not immediately or easily accessible. Think about where you spend the most time in your classroom. That area should be farthest from the entry point to the room. Remember, the farther away a target is from an intruder, the safer that target is.

Use tables, computer carts, book shelves, etc. to create as long as possible route from the door to your location. This provides time. Remember, the more time we have, the greater our chance to survive. If the intruder has to close the distance through a circuitous route to get to you, the class has a better chance of recognizing, assessing, and responding to the threat. Below is a diagram to give you an idea of this concept.

You should always keep your door locked as well. While this is obviously not convenient nor a guarantee against being attacked, it does provide a barrier that must be dealt with. A locked door will provide you with more time. It also helps eliminate some of the element of surprise.

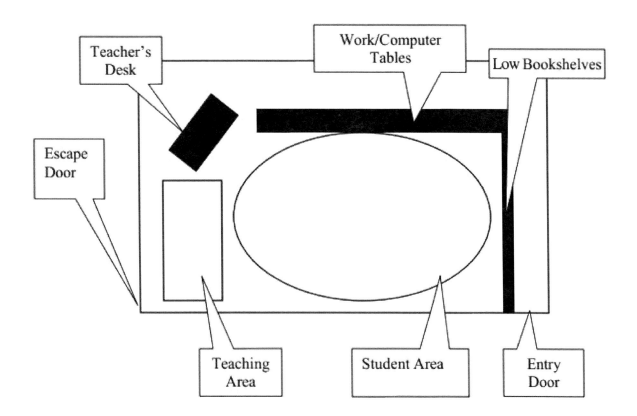

I'm Not Scared...
I'm Prepared!

Objective

Understand and apply the concepts of ALICE

Directions

1. Read the book aloud to students.

2. Have students take turns sharing their favorite part of the book with the group.

3. Have each child draw a picture of their favorite part of the book.

Materials

• Copy of *I'm Not Scared... I'm Prepared* by Julia Cook (National Center For Youth Issues 2014.)
• White construction paper
• Markers, crayons or colored pencils

Show What You Know and "Stick" With IT!

essential

Materials
- Question List
- 17 popsicle sticks
- Container to hold sticks

Objective

Understand and apply the concepts of ALICE

Directions

1. Number popsicle sticks 1-15, leaving two of the sticks blank.

2. Place sticks in container

3. Divide class into two teams.

4. Have a person from Team 1 draw a stick from the container.

5. Match the number on the stick with the corresponding question on the list (page 8) and ask the question.

6. If the question is answered correctly by that person, Team 1 gets to keep the stick. If the question is answered incorrectly, Team 2 can huddle together, decide on an answer, and attempt to answer that question correctly.

7. The team who gets the answer correct, gets to keep the stick.

8. Have a person from Team 2 draw a stick and repeat.

9. If a blank stick is drawn, the team that draws that stick gets to take a stick from the opposing team. (If the opposing team doesn't have any sticks to take, as soon as they earn one, they have to give it to the other team.)

10. When all of the sticks are gone, the team with the most sticks wins!

7

I'm Not Scared…I'm Prepared!
Questions

1. What are some things the teacher prepared her ants for at the Ant Hill School?

ANSWER *Tests, fire drills, bad weather drills, crossing the street, no running in the halls, washing hands, no leaning back in the chairs, watch where you are going*

2. What was the name of the new drill the teacher taught them?

ANSWER *The Sheep, The Shepherd and The Wolf*

3. Why did the teacher teach her ants The Sheep, The Shepherd, and the Wolf Drill?

ANSWER *Any answer having to do with violent intruder*

4. Who is a "dangerous someone"?

ANSWER *Someone in the school who is not supposed to be there*

5. Where was the ants "Special Meeting Place"?

ANSWER *The big tree two blocks away*

6. Where is our "Special Meeting Place" or "Rally Point?"

ANSWER *Answers will vary by school*

7. What did the teacher mean when she said," I am your shepherd and you are my sheep and sheep always do what the shepherd says"?

ANSWER *Obey what the teacher says*

8. When announcements come on, what should all students do?

ANSWER *Stop, Look and Listen to the information*

9. For what does the acronym *ALICE* stand?

ANSWER *Alert, Lockdown, Inform, Counter, Evacuate, and it does not have to go in that order*

10. Describe what students should do during Lockdown.

ANSWER *Be quiet, spread out around the room, stay out of sight, no hiding in places that will restrict movement, be ready to move, have something in your hand to throw, barricade, you may move out of windows (even break windows) to use as a point of escape*

11. How did the teacher tell the ants to move in the hallways?

ANSWER *In a Zig-Zaggy pattern, moving hands, making noise, watch out for and help each other*

12. When the ants get outside, should they wait and run with the teacher to the big tree two blocks away?

ANSWER *No, she said to go and she would meet them there.*

13. What did the ants throw at Mr. Olson, the custodian, when he was playing The Wolf?

ANSWER *Paper wads so they wouldn't hurt him in the drill*

14. Why was the mom ant so surprised when the boy ant told her about ALICE and what they learned?

ANSWER *She couldn't believe he did all he said, because it seemed against the rules.*

15. Why do you think the ants and our class should practice ALICE?

ANSWER *So students will know what to do and be prepared if there is ever a "Dangerous Someone" inside the building.*

Just DO IT!

Materials
- Large plastic clear container
- Ping pong balls (or similar item) – enough to fill the plastic container

Objective

Children will learn how to respond effectively and quickly when given the **STOP, LOOK** and **LISTEN** signal.

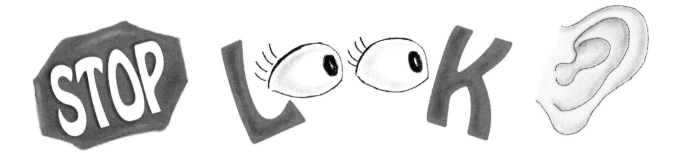

Directions

1. Establish your signal for STOP LOOK and LISTEN (needs to be attention getting signal such as chimes playing, a specific clap, turning off and on the lights etc.)

2. Discuss why it is important to have STOP LOOK and LISTEN signal.

3. Practice using and responding to the signal appropriately with your students.

4. Each time your whole class responds appropriately to the **STOP, LOOK** and **LISTEN** signal, reward them by letting one student place a ping pong ball inside the jar.

5. When the jar is full, celebrate your great response times by offering the class a reward i.e.

- Free assignment pass
- Pizza party
- Lunch on the lawn
- Extra computer time

NOTE It is important to establish what the class reward will be prior to starting this activity, so that the students will know what they are working for. You may wish to offer numerous possibilities for rewards that children can vote on when the jar is full, but they need to know what the choices are in advance.

Practice often and keep expectations high. This is one area a teacher should NOT compromise standards and expectations. Keep in mind however, once established, careless overuse/abuse of a STOP LOOK and LISTEN signal leads to under effectiveness.

essential

"STICK"er With Doing the Right Thing!

Objective

Children will learn how to respond effectively and quickly when given the **STOP, LOOK and LISTEN** signal.

Directions

1. Each time you give the signal for **STOP, LOOK and LISTEN**, reward 3-5 students who respond quickly and effectively by giving them a sticky label that they can write their name on and wear.

2. At the end of the day, have students take their labels off and stick them up on the bulletin board in recognition of their actions.

3. Let the stickers build up throughout the year until the entire bulletin board is covered with evidence of great STOP LOOK and LISTENERS!!!

Optional Activity

Instead of having students stick labels up on a bulletin board, form a ball of old labels that keeps growing and growing. See how big your label ball can get by the end of the school year!

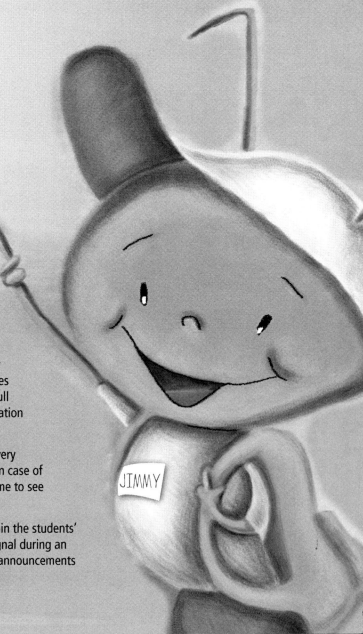

NOTE: It is critical that students be expected to listen to the teacher or important information and follow directions as told, without asking questions, such as "Why?" The older the student, the more examples of "Why" this is important can be explained by the teacher. An Alert may come through the public address system, or it may be through their senses if the intruder is close enough. Therefore, students must train on giving full attention when the teacher gives information or the signal. Good information makes for good decision-making.

Classrooms are places of learning and learning can be noisy; however, every teacher should be able to gain immediate attention from their students in case of an emergency. Hopefully, as the drills are practiced, the students will come to see the value very quickly, no matter their age.

Many teachers already have "Attention" hand signals or cue words to gain the students' immediate attention. If so, the teacher can just explain that this is the signal during an emergency also. Expand the expectation of Stop, Look and Listen when announcements from the office come on also, if the students do not already do so.

essential

Let's Take a Walk!

Objective

Students will learn where their "Special Meeting Place" or rally point is and figure out the best route to get there.

Directions

1. Take your class on a walking field trip and visit your school's rally point. Depending on the location, decide if there are multiple ways to reach the rally point, and if it is feasible to teach the students different ways to get there.

2. Emphasize to students that during an actual emergency or ALICE drill, they will run to the rally point and WILL NOT need to wait for a teacher to lead them.

3. Invite parents to meet you at the rally point so students and parents will know where to go in case of an emergency.

4. Send a letter home explaining that in the case of an evacuating emergency, parents and guardians should plan to meet their children and school officials at the rally point, NOT at the school. Make sure to include safety release requirements and procedures in the letter.

5. Invite the fire department and/or local law enforcement agencies to meet you at the rally point so that students will see that the flashing lights on the first responder vehicles are signs of help. This is a great opportunity for first responders to reinforce their roles as community leaders.

6. Ask older students (4th, 5th, and 6th graders) to walk on the field trip with the younger students. In an actual emergency, older students may be very helpful to younger students.

7. Throughout the year, random students should be asked by adults in the building: "If we have an emergency and you have to leave the building, with or without the teacher, where do you go? Where is our school's "Special Meeting Place?"

Our Special Meeting Place
(Establishing a Rally Point)

It is vital that schools establish a "special meeting place" or "rally point" away from but within a safe walking distance of a school so that if ever a "dangerous someone" is in the building, and you need to evacuate, everyone knows where to go. The rally point location should be decided collaboratively by law enforcement and school district officials. Once a rally point has been established, it is imperative that students, teachers, and parents know where the rally point is located, and be able to recognize the most direct route to that rally point.

Our Special Meeting Place!

Objective

Students will become aware of where the school's rally point is located, and learn the most direct path to that rally point.

Directions

Take a photo of the special meeting place with the school in the background. Enlarge the photo and hang it up on your classroom wall with **OUR SPECIAL MEETING PLACE** written below the photo.

Our Special Meeting Place!

My Map of Our Special Meeting Place

SCHOOL

MEETING PLACE

Materials

- Construction paper
- Markers, colored pencils, or crayons

Objective

Students will become aware of where the school's rally point is located, and learn the most direct path to that rally point.

Directions

Have each student draw and color a map of the school, the special meeting place and the most direct path connecting the two.

essential

12

Exit Awareness

Objective

Recognize and locate all of the exits in the building.

Directions

1. Create a map of your school and make a copy for each child and create one larger version of the map for the teacher to display in the class.

2. Take your class on a walking field trip around the inside of your school, and have them draw exit signs on their maps with green markers as you locate the exits throughout the building.

3. You do the same on your larger map.

4. Display your map on the wall of your classroom for all to see.

5. Have adults in the building periodically ask students, "Where is the closest exit to us right now?"

The Lockdown Great 8!

Materials
- Classroom setting and students
- To Do list
- Pen or pencil

Objective
Students will understand the concept of LOCKDOWN and know what they need to do to respond effectively.

Directions

1. Discuss each step of **LOCKDOWN** in detail, and have students write down the steps in order on their to do lists as they are discussed:

- **Stop, Look, Listen**
- **Lock the door**
- **Turn out the lights**
- **Push desks and other furniture up against the door**
- **Tie leg of desk to door knob with durable chord**
- **Place large zip tie around top opening arm**
- **Grab your special something**
- **Spread out in the classroom away from the door and out of sight, but make sure you have enough room to move**

2. Practice doing the Great 8 several times.

3. Time each practice and try to decrease your time with each try.

To Do List

_____

_____

_____

_____

_____

_____

_____

_____

_____

_____

_____

_____

essential

If The Wolf Gets Into Our Classroom...

Objective

Students will understand the effectiveness of distraction.

Directions

Materials
- A "something "(pencil box, shoe, plastic toy, tissue box) to hold in your hand.
- Wadded up paper balls (three per student)
- Empty chair

1. Review the section of the story, "I'm Not Scared Cause I'm Prepared," when the ants have "somethings" in their hands to hold and throw.

2. Have each student quickly find a "something" they can hold and throw, spread out, and then move to a concealed spot.

3. While standing in their spots, let each student share their "something" and describe why they chose it.

4. Replace students' "something" with three paper wad balls.

5. Set a trash can by the door and on the count of 3 have everyone throw ONE paper wad at the trash can.

6. Discuss: How far did your paper wad ball go? If the trash can was a Wolf, would your paper wad ball have hit the Wolf? Do you think your "something" that you had in your hand previously would have hit the Wolf?

7. Ask for a volunteer or another adult to be the Wolf at the door. Explain to the students that when the Wolf comes through the door they are to throw one paper wad ball at him/her.

8. Give the signal for the Wolf to enter and let the students throw ONE paper wad ball.

9. When the demonstration is finished, ask the volunteer, "What did you see? Could you pick out anyone in particular? Ask the students what they experienced or felt.

10. Ask the volunteer or adult to go back into the hall.

11. Once he/she is out of the room, explain to the students that this time, when the volunteer comes in, you want them to throw their last paper wad ball, and then move to another location of the room.

12. Address any obvious safety issues.

13. Give the signal and let the demonstration happen.

14. Now, ask the same questions to the Wolf and the students.

15. Discuss any issues the students bring up and make any needed adjustments.

16. Remind students if a real Wolf were to enter the classroom, they would throw their "somethings" instead of the paper wad balls. They may also need to throw more than one something to ruin the Wolf's day, so they can run through the doorway or climb out the window.

essential

Run In A Funny ZIG-ZAGGY!

Objectives

- Students will discover the visual skills and concentration it requires to follow a moving object or person.
- Students will develop better body and spatial awareness to make movement in confined areas more efficient and effective.

Materials

Movie clip http://video. nationalgeographic.com/video/ animals/bugs-animals/ants-and-termites/ant_war/

Directions

1. Show a YouTube Movie Clip http://video.nationalgeographic.com/video/animals/bugs-animals/ants-and-termites/ant_war/ (Or teachers should choose a movie clip from YouTube or other resources which shows a close-up of ants moving on the ant hill.)

2. While students are viewing the movie clip, discuss the following points:
   - Can you keep your eye on just one ant and follow them around?
   - See if the ant you are watching runs into or walks over another ant?
   - Do you think ants talk to one another?
   - Do you think ants work together as a team?
   - What do you think ants would learn if they went to Ant School?

TEACHERS Keep in mind and review all safety issues or rules needed for the age and ability group.

3. Take the students to the playground or large open area.

4. Instruct students to walk around like the ants being very careful not to run into other "ants".

5. Move the perimeter closer as the students become aware of their bodies, movement, and safe speed. Stress to the students to move quickly like ants without running into one another.

6. Continue to move the perimeter in until the students cannot move without bumping into one another.

7. Then move the students back into the classroom and see if they can safely move out of the room without running into one another.

8. Have the students exit the classroom through the door, and move down the hall walking quickly in a zig-zaggy pattern to the nearest exit, stopping right outside the door.

9. Estimate with the students how long it took to get everyone out (without any collisions) WALKING quickly only.

10. Repeat the drill using a stopwatch to calculate the exact time for all to exit.

11. Compare the estimate with the actual time.

12. Explain that during an actual emergency, students need to carefully run zig-zaggy (as opposed to walking quickly) out of the building.

essential

Match Game

Directions

Answer each question below using the best answer. On the ant teacher's blackboard, write the letter of the answer in the box above the number of the question to discover a hidden message.

1. **What does the acronym ALICE stand for?**
    B. *Accept, Like, Impress, Care, Esteem*
    E. *Alert, Lockdown, Inform, Counter, Evacuate*
    G. *After, Looking, Inward, Cry, Elephant*

2. **When the ants get outside, should they wait and run with the teacher to the big tree two blocks away?**
    R. *Maybe, it depends on how much time they have before lunch*
    Q. *Yes, they could get lost*
    P. *No, she said to go and she would meet them there*

3. **Who is a "dangerous someone"?**
    L. *An upset teacher*
    D. *You're neighbor's new puppy*
    N. *Someone in the school who is not supposed to be there*

4. **What are some of the things the teacher prepared her ants for at the Ant Hill School?**
    I. *Tests, fire drills, bad weather drills, crossing the street, no running in the halls, washing hands, no leaning back in the chairs, watch where you are going*
    J. *How to drive a truck, work a vending machine, pick out coordinating colors*
    C. *Whistling in tune, show business, juggling, life in the circus, stand up comedy*

5. **Why was the mom ant so surprised when the boy ant told her about ALICE and what they learned?**
    Z. *Her middle name is ALICE*
    R. *She couldn't believe he did all he said, because it seemed against the rules*
    X. *She thought ALICE was a new student*

continued on next page

6. **Where was the ants "special meeting place"?**

    A. *The big tree two blocks away*

    T. *Principal's Office*

    H. *Papa Ant's Pizza Parlor*

7. **Why did the teacher teach her ants The Sheep, The Shepherd, and the Wolf Drill?**

    A. *To keep them safe or get them to safety quickly in case of an intruder emergency*

    O. *So they could understand the story of "Little Red Riding Hood" better*

    W. *So they would be prepared for the school play*

8. **Describe what students should do during Lockdown.**

    X. *Be quiet, spread out around the room, stay out of sight, no hiding in places that will restrict movement, be ready to move, have something in your hand to throw, barricade, you may move out of windows (even break windows) to use as a point of escape*

    S. *Make as much noise as possible so everyone knows where you are*

    Z. *Finish your homework then discuss what you'll do after school with your friends*

9. **When announcements come on, what should all students do?**

    U. *Request their favorite song*

    C. *Stop, Look and Listen to the information*

    W. *Salute and stand at attention*

10. **What did the ant teacher mean when she said," I am your shepherd and you are my sheep, and sheep always do what the shepherd says"?**

    I. *Obey what the teacher says so she can keep you safe*

    F. *She liked to talk about sheep*

    V. *She really wanted to have a sheep farm, but couldn't afford one*

11. **What did the ants throw at Mr. Olson, the custodian, when he was playing The Wolf?**

    P. *Cheesy puffs*

    I. *Water balloons*

    E. *Paper wads so they wouldn't hurt him in the drill*

12. **Why do you think the ants and our class should practice ALICE?**

    T. *So students will know what to do and be prepared if there is ever a "Dangerous Someone" inside the building*

    R. *It's a good exercise workout and helps you stay in shape*

    D. *To stay up-to-date with the latest fads*

13. **How did the teacher tell the ants to move in the hallways?**

    I. *Like they're riding a horse*

    E. *In a Zig-Zaggy pattern, moving hands, making noise, watch out for and help each other*

    J. *Do the Electric Slide to the left and to the right*

14. **Which are good examples of a "Special Meeting Place" or "Rally Point?"**

    N. *Your best friend's house*

    G. *Hallway, Classroom Door, Principal's Office*

    L. *A safe place far away from the school (Church, Store, Fire Station, etc.)*

15. **What was the name of the new drill the teacher taught them?**

    K. *Three Little Pigs*

    M. *The Sheep, The Shepherd and The Wolf*

    Q. *Alice in Wonderland*

The Gifts of Being Prepared

Materials
- Gift diagram
- Markers, colored pencils, or crayons
- Scissors
- Shoe box bottom wrapped up and decorated like a gift with a brightly colored *ALICE* printed on the outside of the box

Objective

Understand and apply the concepts of ALICE

Directions

1. Explain that ALICE is the gift of being prepared for a "dangerous someone," but there are many other gifts that students have been given to help them prepare for life.

2. Have each student cut out and decorate their gift diagram and write on the tag what they think is inside (a gift that has been given to help them by a caring someone to prepare them for life (i.e. strong work ethic, math skills, study skills, organization, time management skills etc.)

3. Attach the decorated ALICE gift to bulletin board and place the other gifts around it. Title the board, "The Many Gifts of Being Prepared for LIFE!"

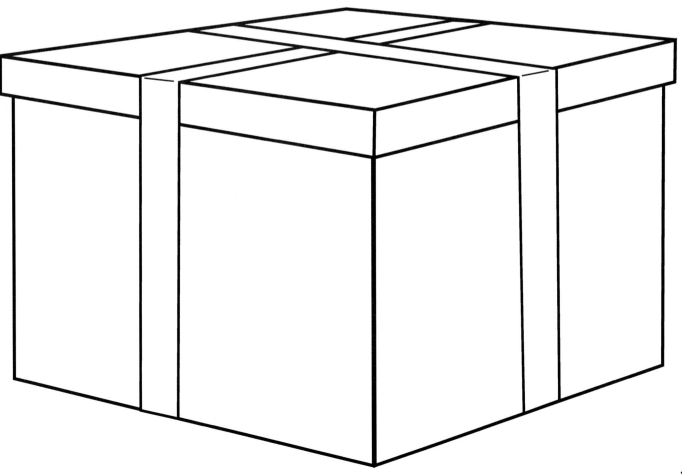

Jigsaw ALICE!

Great plan of action = ALICE

Materials
- 6-8 100 piece jigsaw puzzles
- 4 large poster boards cut in half
- Colored markers
- 6-8 plastic quart sized zip-lock plastic bags

Objective

Understand and apply the concepts of ALICE

Directions

1. Select one child who claims to be good at doing jigsaw puzzles and allow that person to be a team of one.

2. Divide the rest of the class into teams of four.

3. Pass out puzzles, markers and two pieces of cardboard to each team.

4. Have teams work together to complete their puzzles on top of one of the cardboard pieces. (ALL TEAMS MUST START AT THE SAME TIME!)

5. Listen and write down cooperative phrases that you hear from each team (i.e. Great job! Way to go! You do that part and I will work on this etc.)

6. When puzzles are completed, compliment the teams by reflecting upon the positive comments that you overheard.

7. The person who worked alone, will be way behind the others. This is a great time to explain the "Together we are STRONG!" concept. Then have one child from each team join the team of one child and help him/her complete the last puzzle.

8. When all puzzles are completed, have each team place their other piece of cardboard on top of the puzzle and flip it over so that the back of the completed puzzle is showing.

9. Have each team decorate the back of their puzzle with the ALICE acronym, using colored markers:

A Alert
L Lockdown
I Inform
C Counter
E Evacuate

10. Have each team take apart their completed ALICE puzzles and place them in the plastic bag. Allow teams to trade puzzles, select a different solo team player and repeat – reiterating that "Together, We Are STRONG."

Pick the Question. Draw the Answer!

Materials
- Blank construction paper folded in half (one sheet per child)
- Markers, colored pencils or crayons
- Numbered craft sticks (1-15)
- Container for craft sticks
- *I'm Not Scared...I'm Prepared!* question list (See page 8)

Objective

Understand and apply the concepts of ALICE

Directions

1. Using the craft sticks, have each person draw a number and match that number up with a question from the question list.

2. Have each person write out his/her question on the left side of the paper using marker so that it is easily readable.

3. Have each person draw a picture of the answer on the right side of the paper.

4. Display the questions and answers on a bulletin board for all to enjoy.

Design an ALICE T-shirt!

Objective

Understand and apply the concepts of ALICE

Materials

- T-shirt diagram below
- Markers, crayons or colored pencils

Directions

You work for ALICE Training Institute and they have asked you to design a T-shirt for their program that all kids would like to wear. Use the template below to design your T-shirt. Make sure you use the ALICE acronym in your design!

A – Alert   L – Lockdown   I – Inform   C – Counter   E – Evacuate

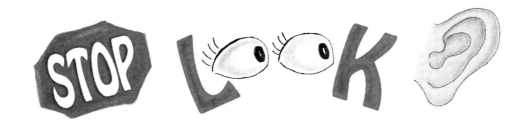

STOP, LOOK and LISTEN Mobile

Objective

Understand the meaning and purpose of **STOP, LOOK and LISTEN**

Directions

1. Have students colorfully write the word **STOP** on one side of the first index card and then on then on the back of that card, have them draw a picture that represents "**STOP**."

2. Repeat this with the other two cards using "**LOOK**" and "**LISTEN**."

3. Punch holes in the cards as shown and string the holes with yarn.

4. Attach the yarn to the hanger and hang mobiles up for display.

Materials

- 1 wire hanger per student
- Paper hole punch
- 5"x 8" unlined index cards (3 per student)
- Yarn
- Markers, Colored Pencils, or Crayons

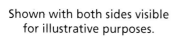

Shown with both sides visible for illustrative purposes.

23

Tell Me All About It!

Objective

In order to fully understand ALICE, you must be able to explain it to others correctly.

Materials
- ALICE info sheet
  See page 3 of this activity guide.
- Signature sheet
- Pen or pencil

Directions

1. Choose five people (preferably grown-ups) and let them read over the ALICE info sheet.

2. Explain ALICE to each person in your own words.

3. Allow the person to ask you questions.

1

Date _____

Signature _____

Printed Name _____

2

Date _____

Signature _____

Printed Name _____

3

Date _____

Signature _____

Printed Name _____

4

Date _____

Signature _____

Printed Name _____

5

Date _____

Signature _____

Printed Name _____